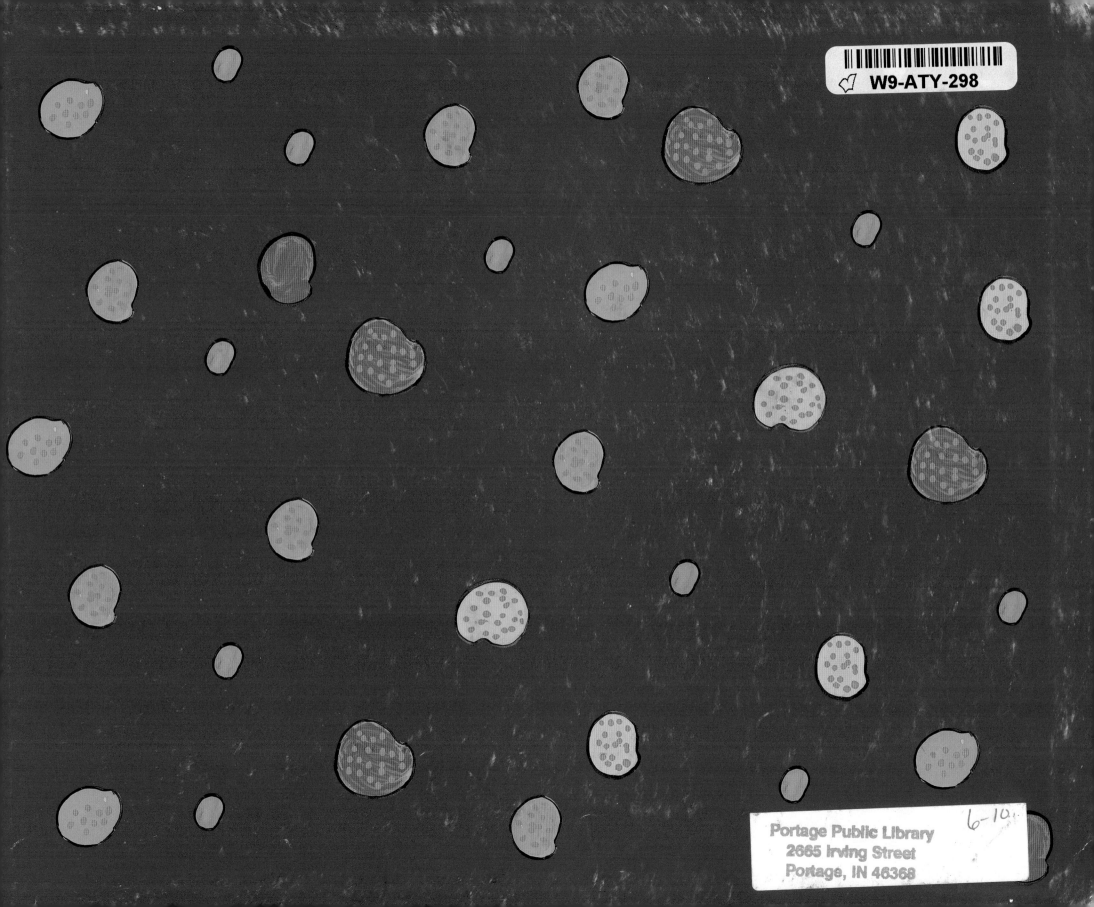

First published in the United States, Great Britain, Canada, Australia, and New Zealand in 2009
by North-South Books Inc., an imprint of NordSüd Verlag AG, CH-8005 Zürich, Switzerland.
Distributed in the United States by North-South Books Inc., New York 10001.

Library of Congress Cataloging-in-Publication Data is available.
ISBN: 978-0-7358-2254-2 (trade edition).
10 9 8 7 6 5 4 3 2 1
Printed in Belgium

www.northsouth.com

John Kilaka

# The Amazing Tree

NorthSouth
New York / London

**Long, long ago,** when the animals had just begun learning to live together, there came a season when no rain fell. The earth was dry, and famine spread throughout the land.

In the middle of this dry land, there stood an amazing tree. Its fruits were ripe and juicy; but as hard as the animals shook the tree, the fruits did not fall.

The fruits were so high up that even the giraffe could not reach them.

"How can we get these fruits?" the hungry animals asked one another.

"I will go ask wise Tortoise," said Rabbit. "He will know what to do."

"Excellent idea," the other animals agreed. "But you are too small to go. You will just forget what wise Tortoise tells you. The big animals must go!"

So it was Elephant and Water Buffalo who went to find wise Tortoise.

It took some time to reach Tortoise's home, but at last Elephant and Water Buffalo arrived.

"Please help us, wise Tortoise," they said. "We are very hungry. We have a tree with fruit that would feed us all, but the fruits will not drop. What should we do to get the fruits?"

"Ah, yes, I know that tree," said Tortoise. "You can only get its fruit if you call the tree by its name. I see you are very hungry, so I will tell you the tree's name. Listen carefully, Elephant. You are old enough to remember this. The name of the tree is Ntunguru meng'enye."

"Thank you, wise Tortoise," said Elephant and Water Buffalo; and they set off for home with the tree's name.

But on the way home, Elephant stumbled and fell. Now, an elephant is very large; and when he falls, it is not always easy for him to get up. By the time Elephant was on his feet again, he had forgotten the name of the tree.

"Do you remember the tree's name?" he asked Water Buffalo.

"Me?" said Water Buffalo. "I don't remember! You are the one wise Tortoise told to listen carefully."

"I did listen carefully," said Elephant. "But when I fell, I forgot the name."

And so Elephant and Water Buffalo returned home without the important name.

The other animals were very disappointed to hear that Elephant had forgotten the tree's name!

"How could you forget something so important?" they cried.

You can imagine how upset they were.

"I will go ask wise Tortoise," said Rabbit; but again the other animals told her, "You are too small." Instead they sent Rhino, Giraffe, and Zebra.

"We are very sorry for disturbing you again," Rhino told wise Tortoise, "but Elephant and Water Buffalo forgot the name. Please tell it to us again."

"They forgot such a simple name? How could that be?" said Tortoise. "Well, I will tell it to you again then. But this time, you should sing it all the way home so you don't forget it." Then he spoke the tree's name very clearly, "Ntunguru meng'enye."

"Thank you very much," said Rhino, Giraffe, and Zebra; and they set off toward home.

As wise Tortoise had suggested, they all sang "Ntunguru meng'enye, Ntunguru meng'enye" to themselves as they walked.

But then Giraffe caught sight of a few green leaves. "Wait a minute while I eat these," she told the others.

"There is no time for that!" said Rhino.

"You mustn't stop singing the tree's name!" said Zebra.

And just like that, they had all stopped singing the name. By the time Giraffe had finished the leaves, none of them could remember it.

And so Rhino, Giraffe, and Zebra returned home without the important name.

"We can't believe this!" said the other animals. "How could all three of you forget this name?" They were very angry. "Who shall we send now?"

"I will go," said Rabbit; but once again the other animals told her, "You are too small." Instead they sent Lion and Leopard.

"Please forgive us for disturbing you again, wise Tortoise," said Lion. "Our friends all forgot the name; but we will not forget it, we promise."

"How could they all forget?" said Tortoise. "This name is not so difficult." He was feeling a bit impatient now. "Well, I will tell you the name again. When you are under the tree, just say 'Ntunguru meng'enye' and the fruits will start dropping down."

"That is all?" said Lion and Leopard. "Let us go then, before we forget it." And they dashed off toward home. "Thank you, wise Tortoise!" they called after them.

On the way home, Lion suddenly froze. Something was rustling in the bush. Lion, the old hunter, turned off the path and vanished into the grassland following the sound. But he could not find anything, so he returned to the path and they continued on their journey.

"Hey Leopard, you remember that name, don't you?" said Lion. "I seem to have forgotten it."

"You startled me so much that I forgot it," said Leopard. "Why did you let yourself get distracted?"

And so Lion and Leopard returned home without the important name.

Now the small animals got very angry. "You big animals are no help at all!" they said. "First you would not let Rabbit go. Then you all came back and had forgotten the name. And meanwhile, we are all starving! We tell you—*this* time Rabbit will go!"

There was nothing much the big animals could say, and so everyone agreed to send Rabbit.

When Rabbit reached Tortoise's house, she knocked on the door.

"Come in, please," said Tortoise, a little surprised to see yet another animal so soon.

"Excuse me for disturbing you," said Rabbit. "I have come for the name because everyone who came before forgot it."

"They all forgot?" said Tortoise a little impatiently. "And now it is you, little Rabbit. Will you remember the name?"

"I will," said Rabbit.

"All right, my little friend; but this is the last time. If *you* forget, then do not send anyone else," said Tortoise. "When you get home, you simply say 'Ntunguru meng'enye,' and the tree will drop its fruits."

"That's all?" said Rabbit. "I can't believe they all forgot it!"

"Neither can I," said Tortoise.

When Rabbit got home, her friends were weak with hunger.

"I've brought the name of the tree!" said Rabbit. "Now stand aside. Once I say its name, the fruit will fall like rain, and you could get hurt."

"Stop talking and call the name!" said the big animals, who didn't really believe that Rabbit could remember it.

So Rabbit called, "Ntunguru meng'enye! Ntunguru meng'enye!"

And the fruits started falling like rain!

UWAAAAAA!

What a feast! The animals ate as much as they could; and when they wanted more, Rabbit called again, "Ntunguru meng'enye!" and more fruits fell from the tree.

The big animals thanked Rabbit. "We have learned a lesson," they said. "We should have trusted you in the first place! Now we know that everyone is important here, no matter whether they are big or small."

And from then on, the animals always had enough to eat.

## ABOUT THIS STORY

This story comes from the Fipa tribe of southwest Tanzania. It was told to me and recorded in the Fipa language (my native tongue) on July 2, 2007. I then translated it into Kiswahili. From Kiswahili, my son, Kilaka Kenny, translated it into simple English. It was then adapted into reading English by NorthSouth Books.

## COLLECTING AFRICAN FOLKTALES

Finding stories isn't as easy as it sounds. When I first started collecting stories, I set out on foot every day at dawn. I could walk for hours before I found a storyteller. The land of the Fipa tribe is in a region of Tanzania called Sumbawanga, which borders Lake Tanganyika. Apart from a few pickup trucks in the summer, there is little transport. People must walk, often for hours, to get where they want to go. Eventually I rented a bike so I could get around more quickly.

The culture of telling stories is disappearing, so not many people know the stories anymore. But on a lucky day, you will find a storyteller, and then you will enjoy listening to amazing stories.

John Kilaka
January 2009

**John Kilaka** was born in Sumbawanga, Tanzania. As a young child, he drew pictures in the sand. When he started school, he felt lucky to find paper and pencils—and colored chalk. Whenever there was any room on the blackboard, he drew pictures there. His classmates loved them; his teachers did not!

In 1987, John moved from his village to Dar es Salaam, where he studied with artist Peter Martin at the village museum, then created his own style of art, now called the Kilaka style. John has traveled around Tanzania collecting stories (*The Amazing Tree* is one of them); participated in storytelling programs in Tanzania, Germany, and Switzerland; and written and illustrated three books.

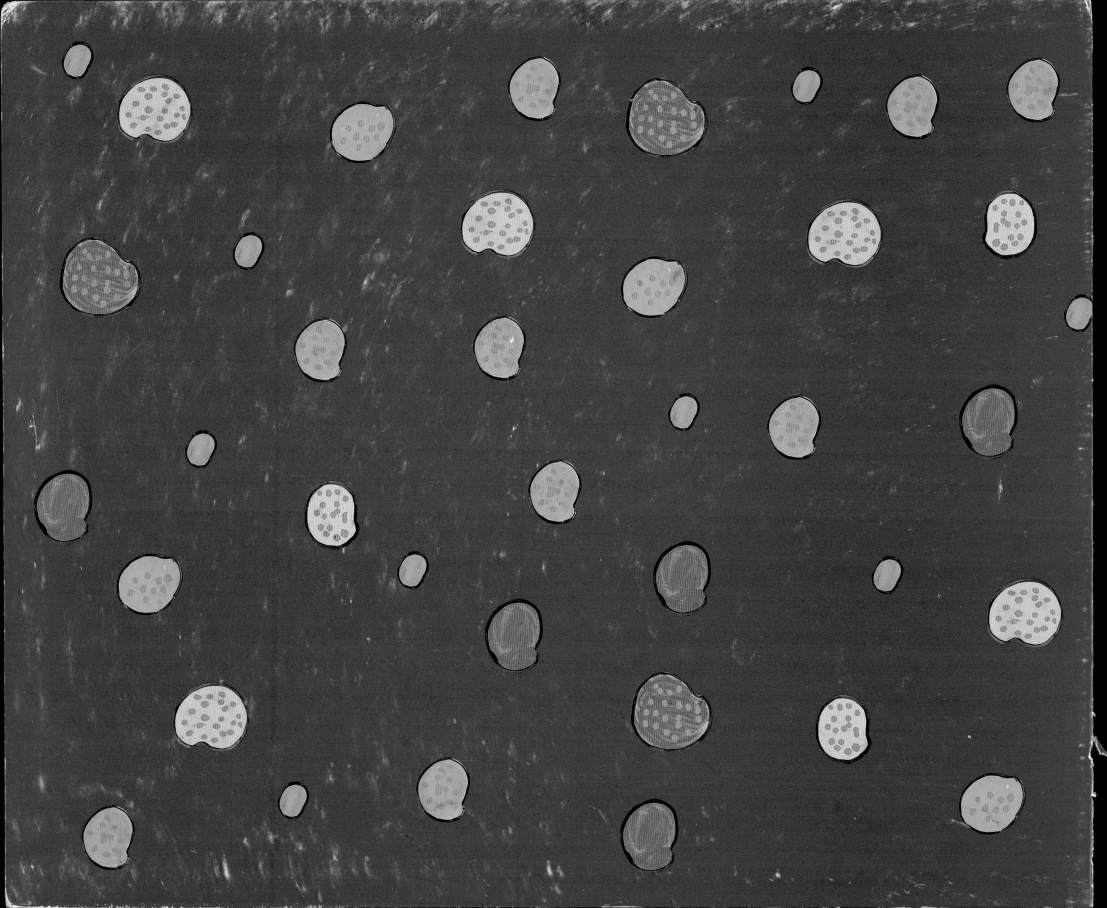